Roll Over Roly

Anne Fine was born and educated in the Midlands, and now lives in County Durham. She has written numerous highly acclaimed and prize-winning books for children and adults. Her novel *The Tulip Touch* won the Whitbread Children's Book of the Year Award; *Goggle-Eyes* won the *Guardian* Children's Fiction Award and the Carnegie Medal, and was adapted for television by the BBC; *Flour Babies* won the Carnegie Medal and the Whitbread Children's Book of the Year Award; *Bill's New Frock* won a Smarties Prize, and *Madame Doubtfire* has become a major feature film.

www.annefine.co.uk

ANNE FINE

Roll Over Roly

Illustrated by Philippe Dupasquier

PUFFIN BOOKS

For Sonia Benster's dad

PUFFIN BOOKS

Published by the Penguin Group
Penguin Books Ltd, 80 Strand, London WC2R ORL, England
Penguin Putnam Inc., 375 Hudson Street, New York, New York 10014, USA
Penguin Books Australia Ltd, 250 Camberwell Road, Camberwell, Victoria 3124, Australia
Penguin Books Canada Ltd, 10 Alcorn Avenue, Toronto, Ontario, Canada M4V 3B2
Penguin Books India (P) Ltd, 11 Community Centre, Panchsheel Park, New Delhi – 110 017, India
Penguin Books (NZ) Ltd, Cnr Rosedale and Airborne Roads, Albany, Auckland, New Zealand
Penguin Books (South Africa) (Pty) Ltd, 24 Sturdee Avenue, Rosebank 2196, South Africa

Penguin Books Ltd, Registered Offices: 80 Strand, London WC2R ORL, England

www.penguin.com

First published 1999
9

Text copyright © Anne Fine, 1999
Illustrations copyright © Philippe Dupasquier, 1999
All rights reserved

The moral right of the author and illustrator has been asserted

Set in Baskerville MT

Printed in England by Clays Ltd, St Ives plc

Except in the United States of America, this book is sold subject to the condition that it shall not,
by way of trade or otherwise, be lent, re-sold, hired out, or otherwise circulated without the
publisher's prior consent in any form of binding or cover other than that in which it is published and
without a similar condition including this condition being imposed on the subsequent purchaser

British Library Cataloguing in Publication Data
A CIP catalogue record for this book is available from the British Library

ISBN 0–141–30318–2

Contents

1 Take the Road of Not Yet

RUPERT'S MOTHER AND father had
to go to Great Uncle Percy's funeral.
All the usual babysitters were busy.
So Rupert was dropped off at Great
Aunt Ada's house, with Roly, his
puppy.

Rupert and Great Aunt Ada waved
the car round the corner, while Roly
sat in a wet flower bed.

"You knew Great Uncle Percy," said
Rupert. "Why aren't you going too?"

"No fear!" said Great Aunt Ada. "At
my age, funerals in wet weather tend to
be catching."

She turned to see Roly sprawling about in her pansies.

"Out!" she said. "Out of there at once!"

Roly ignored her, and began to chew a begonia.

"Isn't he trained yet?" Great Aunt Ada asked Rupert crossly.

"Not yet," Rupert admitted. He didn't
want to admit to someone he hardly
knew that his new puppy was so round
and warm and soft and lovely that he
couldn't bring himself even to start to be
a little firm.

So he just said again, "Not yet. I keep
meaning to start, but I never get round
to it."

Great Aunt Ada frowned at him over
the top of her spectacles.

"Take the Road of Not Yet," she
warned, "and the only place you'll arrive
is the Land of Never."

Then she gave Roly a sharp poke with
her walking stick, and he shot off the
flower bed at once.

"That's better," said Great Aunt Ada.
"After all, rather unborn than untaught."
And she led the way back up the path to
her little house.

Rupert trailed after her while Roly

raced ahead, barking. In the front room, there was a glossy green parrot in a large wire cage.

"Now, *there*," said Great Aunt Ada, "is a pet to make an owner *proud*."

Rupert was embarrassed for Roly. But Roly just kept skittering about, making a nuisance of himself and jumping on furniture.

Inside the cage, the parrot sat silently on its perch, blinking at Rupert with a beady eye.

Rupert went closer.

"Hello, Polly," he said to the parrot. "Hello, Polly."

"Gordon," Great Aunt Ada corrected. "The parrot's name is Gordon."

"Hello, Gordon," said Rupert.

The parrot opened its beak. "Faster!" it shouted. "Faster, you dozy lump! Faster!"

Startled, Rupert backed away, and Roly stopped barking and stared.

"Gordon belonged to Great Uncle Percy," Great Aunt Ada explained to Rupert. "Your mother wasn't madly keen, so he came here instead."

"I see," said Rupert.

"Jump!" screeched the parrot. "Get on with it! Jump! Jump!"

Poor Roly whined in terror and

scratched at the door, desperate to get away.

"Was Great Uncle Percy a very rude man?" Rupert couldn't help asking.

"No," said Great Aunt Ada, mystified. "Why on earth should you think that?"

"No reason," Rupert said hastily. "Honestly, no reason."

"Go!" screeched the parrot. "Stop hanging about like an old lady! Go, go, *go*!"

Great Aunt Ada looked just the tiniest bit put out. "We'll leave Gordon in peace, shall we?" she said loftily. "Let's go into the kitchen."

Rupert followed her willingly.

"Rubbish!" the parrot called after them. "Absolute rubbish!"

2 All Uncooked Joints
Will be Carved

UP AT THE table, Rupert piled his plate high with slices of the cake his mother had left with them.

"It was too early for breakfast when we left home," he explained, steadying his elbows on Great Aunt Ada's flowery tablecloth as he took his first huge bite.

"I see you're as poorly trained as your dog," Great Aunt Ada said tartly. "I warn you, all uncooked joints on this table will be carved."

Hastily, Rupert took his elbows off the table.

"That's better," said Great Aunt Ada.

Roly raced round and round the chair legs, hoping that cake crumbs would fall.

Great Aunt Ada scolded him. "Behave, or you'll go in the broth pot!"

Rupert sighed. His mother had warned him. "Don't worry about Great Aunt Ada. Her bark's worse than her bite." But still, it was going to be a very long day – for himself and for Roly.

He finished the cake. Then, "I think I'll just slip off and play quietly on my own now," he said, sliding down from the table.

Great Aunt Ada gazed up at the ceiling and chanted a little rhyme.

"The little boy who did not say
'Thank you' and 'If you please'
Was scraped to death with oyster shells
Under the coconut trees."

Rupert took the hint.

"Please," he said. "Please may I get down from the table and go and play?"

"Yes," said Great Aunt Ada. "Yes, you may."

"And thank you for the lovely cake," Rupert added, even though his own mother had brought it. (Better to be on the safe side.)

"Not at all," Great Aunt Ada said graciously. "It was my pleasure."

As he went out of the door (tripping over Roly), he quite distinctly heard her saying smugly to herself, "Well, there you are. Good manners are like measles. The only way to get them is to spend time where they already are."

3 When Sunny Smile . . .

INSIDE THE BOX his parents had left in
the hall, he found his raincoat and his
boots, his school reading book and Roly's
dog food and dish.

Rupert put his head back round the
door.

"Great Aunt Ada, where's the other
box?"

"What other box?"

"The one with my games and my
jigsaw and my aeroplanes and my
models and glue and my old binoculars
and my giant red magnet and my
football cards and my interactive

dinosaur family and my racing cars and –"

"Your father only carried in one box," Great Aunt Ada interrupted. "And your mother didn't bring in anything, except the cake."

Rupert was horrified. All day. All *day* in Great Aunt Ada's awful, boring, stuffy house. No cassette player. No computer. No television, even. (That's why they'd packed the box.)

And Mum had told him only about a million times, "I *know* Great Aunt Ada isn't going to be the world's greatest babysitter. But, honestly, there's no one else. So be *polite*."

Well, he would try. But not *that* hard.

"I'll manage," he called out, adding a little ungraciously under his breath, "I suppose I'll have to, won't I?"

But she'd appeared in the doorway. She had seen his face.

"Look at you," she said. "You look like a man sent to empty a bath with a teaspoon."

He tried a little smile.

She waited.

He tried harder.

Still she waited.

The next smile came out almost properly.

"That's better," she said. "Never forget:

When Sunny Smile from Castle Gloom
  is freed,
He unlocks Heart, who rushes to the
  lead."

That made him laugh. (Though he had the good manners to wait till she was back in the kitchen.)

4 Don't Boast When You Set Off

IT JUST POPPED out of him.

"I'm bored."

"I'll find you a job," she said promptly, and opened a cupboard door.

Inside was the vacuum cleaner.

"You lift it," she told him. "I'm older, so I'll just do the groaning."

Rupert hauled it out.

"Do this room first," said Great Aunt Ada. "Then go across the hall and do the other room, especially under Gordon's cage. And then, if you're still bored –"

Hastily, Rupert plugged in the vacuum cleaner and switched it on. The noise

15

drowned out her voice, and she went off.
He started vacuuming. He didn't mind.
He quite enjoyed it really – until Great
Aunt Ada came back in again to tell him
to go in straight lines.

"See?" she said, taking the cleaner.
"Up. Down. Up. Down."

"But, *why*?"

"So you can see exactly where you've been."

"But I *remember* where I've been. Mum says I'm really good at vacuuming."

"Don't boast when you set off," said Great Aunt Ada. "Boast when you get there."

Then she went back to the conservatory, and her book.

Rupert pressed on, trying to keep in straight lines, but not let the vacuum cleaner put Roly in so much of a frenzy that he barked, and fetched Great Aunt Ada back in again.

Roly raced round and round, leaping on chairs and crashing into little nests of tables.

"Why don't you just sit quietly on that rug?" Rupert suggested.

Roly ignored him, and skidded into the fireguard.

"Sit!" Rupert told him more sharply.

But Roly just skittered back again.

"Please, Roly," said Rupert. "This is *impossible*."

Roly rushed round even faster, tangling himself in the vacuum-cleaner lead.

"Be a good dog," begged Rupert.

Roly just whined and pawed at Rupert's new trousers. Rupert pushed him down and carried on vacuuming. Up, down, up, down (in case Great Aunt Ada came back in again), over the hall, and into the other room.

Roly raced after him, tangling himself back up in the vacuum-cleaner lead.

"Roll over, Roly!" Rupert told him, unravelling the loops. "Roll over!"

Roly just lay there staring, then raced further into the room.

Spotting the parrot suddenly, he changed his mind, skidded to a halt, and rushed off towards the back door.

"Come *back*," pleaded Rupert over the

whine of the vacuum. "Roly, come
back!" He was worried Roly would chew
more of Great Aunt Ada's begonias. But
Roly paid no attention. He just
pretended that he hadn't heard, and
charged off round the corner.

Rupert gave up, and went back to his
vacuuming.

In the front room, the carpet was a mess. All round the cage were bits of grit Gordon had kicked off his tray, and seed husks he'd spat out.

Rupert turned up the vacuum to full power.

"Faster!" shrieked Gordon over the vacuum's roar.

"Oh, hush!" said Rupert.

"Faster!" the parrot repeated. "Faster, you dozy lump!"

"Be quiet!" Rupert snapped.

"Get on with it!" Gordon snapped back, and swivelled on his perch to keep his eye on the vacuum cleaner as Rupert pushed it up and down. The parrot wasn't helping, Rupert couldn't help noticing. Each time Rupert cleaned a perfect stripe of carpet, he kicked more grit out between the bars, to mess it up again.

Rupert was irritated. "Stop that!" he told Gordon. "How am I supposed to clean up around you if you keep kicking down more?"

Gordon just blinked at him.

Rupert worked faster, up and down. The parrot waited till he'd almost finished, then kicked some more mess out between the bars.

It floated down to the carpet.

"Stop it!" Rupert said sharply. "Just sit and behave, please!"

Still blinking insolently, Gordon kicked more. "Quickly!" he screeched. "Faster! Faster!"

Rupert switched off the vacuum cleaner and put his hands on his hips. "Listen," he told the parrot. "This is not my idea of the perfect day. It's bad enough having Great Aunt Ada telling me what to do and how to do it. 'Make sure you go in straight lines! Up! Down! Up! Down!' But I'm certainly not taking orders from a parrot."

Gordon said nothing. Only blinked at him.

Rupert waited.

Gordon was silent.

Rupert waited some more.

Gordon just blinked.

"Right then," said Rupert. "If that's

fully understood, I'll get on with the
vacuuming."

Just at that moment, Roly's head
appeared at the window.

"*Wheeeeeeeeeeeeeeeeeee!*" Gordon
screeched like an express train.

Roly turned and fled.

"Rubbish!" Gordon squawked contemptuously. "Absolute rubbish!"

He tucked his head under his wing, and refused to come out again.

5 Bad Habits Are First Cobwebs

AN HOUR LATER, it slipped out again:
"I'm bored."

"When I was your age," said Great
Aunt Ada, "I had a box of buttons and a
cotton reel to play with. And I was *never*
bored."

"Blimey!" said Rupert.

"Set a brave soldier to guard that
tongue, young man," Great Aunt Ada
warned. "Bad habits are first cobwebs,
then cables. Haven't you got a book?"

"I've finished it."

"Then I'll find you another job."

This time, it was windows. He enjoyed

that more. She didn't have any of the
fancy blue cleaning sprays his parents
used. She just filled a rattling tin bucket
with warm, soapy water and gave him a
strange, furry leather cloth that felt all
slimy in his hand when it was wet, but
worked like magic. He made the glass

panes sparkle. Rupert worked steadily round the house, window by window, taking care with the china ornaments inside and the flower beds outside.

Roly stayed locked in the kitchen, barking like a fiend.

After a while, Great Aunt Ada poked her head out of one of her freshly gleaming windows, and said, "That dog of yours certainly knows the best way to get in the neighbours' Book of Sinners."

Rupert couldn't help sighing. Much as he adored Roly, the noise was getting on his nerves as well.

"I can't do anything with him," he said forlornly. "He just doesn't care."

Great Aunt Ada said darkly:

"Don't Care was made to care.
Don't Care was hung.
Don't Care was put in a pot
And boiled till he was done."

Rupert was glad that he and Great Aunt Ada had got to know each other a little better. Because it was the second time that day she'd mentioned cooking his pet.

6 Life Is a Splendid Robe

"REST TIME," DECLARED Great Aunt Ada when the plates were cleared away. "Gangplank up. Batten the hatches."

"I don't have rests," said Rupert, quite astonished.

"I do," said Great Aunt Ada, as if that settled it. Rupert remembered his mother's words: "People her age grew up in a different world. They're simply not used to children arguing back. They think it's rude. So, whatever she says, just go along with her, and we'll be back at half-past four to rescue you. It's a promise."

"Right then," Rupert told Great Aunt Ada. "Rest time it is."

She found him one or two things to keep him amused through his quiet time. One was *The Giant Book of Battles*. ("Your Great Uncle Percy lost a finger in that one," she said, pointing at one of the pictures.) And another thing was a kaleidoscope.

"*Brilliant!*" said Rupert, holding it to the light and twisting it to watch the colours tumble from one astonishing pattern to the next. "*Brilliant!*"

"It's one of my best ones," she admitted. "It took me ages."

He stared at her in wonder. "You made this?"

"They're not all that difficult," she told him. "They just take a good deal of care and time. But all you really need is a nice bit of wood, some oil, and shards of coloured glass."

His eyes lit up.

"If I ever have to come again because of a funeral, will you show me how?"

She laughed at him. "Don't be a dilly! The next funeral in this family is likely to be *mine*."

"Oh!" He was startled. "I'm sorry."

"Not to worry," she assured him cheerfully. "That's how it goes. Life is a splendid robe. Its only fault is its short length."

Rupert said shyly, "I could come round and visit you anyway . . ."

"Not till that dog's learned some manners," Great Aunt Ada said.

And left the room.

7 *Roll Over, Roly!*

HE DIDN'T MEAN to fall asleep. He
wasn't really tired. Somewhere, in the
back of his mind, he half-remembered
hearing poor Roly scrabbling desperately
at some closed door, and muffled barks.
But after that, the only thing he heard
was Great Aunt Ada snoring through the
wall when he woke up.

And thumping.

Strange, irregular thumps.

And squawkings. Lifting his head from
the pillow, he could hear squawks.

And more thumps.

More squawks.

Squawk.

Thump.

Squawk.

Thump.

Rupert slid off the bed and crept to the door.

Squawk!

Thump!

He crept along the hall.

Squawk! Thump! Squawk! Thump!

Then silence.

Rupert crept closer and put his ear flat against the door. Inside, he could hear scrabbling, and then his own voice, sharp with irritation.

"Just sit and behave, please!"

The parrot was using his voice. Rupert was astonished. He'd only told Gordon off once – for flicking grit on the carpet. He knew parrots were brilliant at copying noises and voices. But, still, it was *amazing*.

There was another short scrabble.
Then, "Stop that! Sit! Roll over, Roly!"

It was his own voice again, to the life.
The imitation was so perfect that if his
own mother had been standing there
beside the door, she would have thought
that it was him.

Another silence. Then, "Jump, you dozy lump! Up! Down! Faster!"

Rupert could tell from the mixture of voices that this was partly Great Uncle Percy shouting, and partly himself getting ratty about having to push the vacuum cleaner in straight lines.

Then, "Absolute rubbish!" (Great Uncle Percy again.)

More scrabbling. Then, "Roly, come back!" (His own voice.)

A short burst of vacuum cleaner.

One or two express trains.

Then, "Roll over, Roly! Jump! Jump, you dozy lump! Up! Down!"

Now Rupert could hear panting. And a whimper. But, almost at once, he heard his own voice saying through the door, "Oh, hush! Just sit and behave, please!"

Instantly, there was silence through the door. In panic, Rupert pushed it open. And, sure enough, there on the carpet,

looking as limp as Great Aunt Ada's
furry window-washing cloth, was
poor little Roly, tired
out.

"Jump!"
screeched
the parrot
again,
ignoring
Rupert.

Terrified, Roly scrambled to his feet,
and jumped.

"Faster!" yelled Gordon. "Roll over!
Faster! Faster!"

Roly rolled over and jumped, faster
and faster.

Rupert was horrified. "Roly!" he called
out. "Roly!"

Roly spun round
and saw him.
He was
about to

hurl himself across the room into the safety of Rupert's outstretched arms, when Gordon screeched again.

"Just sit and behave, please!"

Instantly, Roly sat.

Rupert called from the doorway. "Come here, Roly."

Gratefully, Roly hurtled across the carpet towards Rupert.

"Roly, come back!" called the parrot, using Rupert's voice.

Instantly, Roly ran back.

Rupert was furious. "Shut up!" he yelled at Gordon. "Just shut up!" He reached out for Roly, who turned to gaze at him with pleading eyes, but didn't dare move till Gordon suddenly snapped, out of the blue, "Stop hanging about like an old lady! Go, go, *go!*"

In a flash, Roly was across the room and safe in Rupert's arms. Rupert held him tight. He could feel his little pet's heart thumping. Furious with Gordon, he shouted at him from the doorway.

"You are the *meanest, nastiest, rudest —*"

Behind him, he heard a soft cough.

Rupert swung round. Great Aunt Ada was in the hallway, looking the picture of innocence and holding a plate of biscuits.

8 Accidents Will Happen

"AFTER MY REST," Great Aunt Ada said, "I usually have a little snack. Do come and join me."

Spotting the biscuits, Roly began struggling in Rupert's arms. Rupert bent down to release him, then turned to give the parrot one last angry look before following Great Aunt Ada into the kitchen.

She was holding the plate at a very slippy angle.

"Careful," he warned. "You're –"

Too late. One of the biscuits slid off on to the floor.

Plop!
Instantly, Roly made a dive for it.
"Sit!" said Great Aunt Ada, without
even turning round.

Roly sat.

Another biscuit dropped.

"Sit!" repeated Great Aunt Ada.

Roly lifted his backside a tiny bit from the floor. For a moment, it trembled. Then he obediently parked it back again.

"There's a good boy," said Great Aunt Ada, and gave Roly a biscuit to reward him.

Rupert stared.

"You try," Great Aunt Ada said, handing Rupert the plate.

"But –"

"Go on. Have a go."

So Rupert had a go. He tipped the plate till yet another biscuit fell on the floor and broke in half. Roly jumped to his feet and set off after one of the bits.

"Sit!" Rupert told him.

Roly sat.

"Excellent!" said Great Aunt Ada. "Let's see what else he's learned." She moved her chair back safely. "Run round the table," she told Rupert. "Get him excited."

"But –"

"Go on."

So Rupert ran round the table, and, almost at once, Roly started after him, barking.

"Be quiet!" said Great Aunt Ada.

Roly fell silent.

"There!" said Great Aunt Ada. "Very good indeed. Dear Gordon has made the most excellent start on his training."

Rupert gave Great Aunt Ada a suspicious look. "You locked poor Roly in there, didn't you?" he accused her. "You did it deliberately. You shut him in there on purpose! All through our rest time!"

"On purpose?" Great Aunt Ada's eyes widened. "Good heavens, Rupert. In these little houses, doors are forever

slamming shut. Accidents will happen."

She held the plate of biscuits out
towards him.

Furious, he ignored it.

She offered it again. "Come along,
Rupert," she told him. "He who is angry
at a feast is rude."

Biscuits were hardly a feast, Rupert
thought bitterly. But, on the other hand,

he didn't want to behave like Gordon the parrot.

Absolutely not.

So, curbing his temper, Rupert reached out for a double-filled chocolate Wagon Wheel with strawberry piping.

And said thanks.

9 *Faster, You Dozy Lump! Faster!*

AND IT WAS wonderful to have a pet
who came when he was called, and
didn't spoil games by jumping up and
barking all the time. First, they played
Trackers through the garden. Then they
played Alien Landing. Then they played
Outlaws on the Run.

And then, before he knew it, his
parents' car was pulling up outside.

Rupert rushed to the gate. Roly ran
after him. As soon as his parents were
out of the car, and looking, Rupert said
proudly to Roly, "Sit!"

And Roly sat.

"Roll over!" said Rupert.

Instantly, Roly rolled over and came up the right way without messing.

"Well!" said his mother, and stared admiringly.

His father said, "Smart idea, Rupert! A good way to spend the day: training Roly!"

Rupert considered. He could just take a bow. (After all, he and Roly had been practising "Sit!" and "Be quiet!" and "Roll over!" all through Trackers and Alien Landing and Outlaws on the Run.)

Or he could tell the truth.

"Well," he admitted. "Great Aunt Ada helped a lot."

He paused, and then added, "And so did Great Uncle Percy."

"Great Uncle Percy?" His mother looked puzzled. "But, Rupert, that's impossible. We've just come back from –"

"I know," said Rupert. "But he did help. Honestly. With his awful rudeness."

"*Rudeness?*" His mother shook her head. "No, Great Uncle Percy was *never* rude. He was the kindest, gentlest, sweetest man."

"That's right," agreed Rupert's father. "I'm sure he never in his whole long life said a cross word."

"You ought to listen to his parrot," Rupert said.

"Gordon? Why, what does Gordon say?"

Rupert was nowhere near as good as a parrot at copying voices. But still, he did his best.

"Quickly!" he yelled. "Jump! Faster, you dozy lump! Stop hanging about like an old lady! Get on with it! Go, go, *go*!"

His parents burst out laughing.

"Oh, well," said his mother. "You have to remember that, till last week, Gordon's cage was sitting right beside Great Uncle Percy's bed."

"In his room in that nursing home beside the railway line."

"Overlooking the racetrack."

Rupert's father was grinning. "It was probably the most exciting moment of the old soul's week."

"Imagine," said Rupert's mother, "if the nurse puts a bet on a horse for you."

"And you can see it running past your window."

"You'd probably start yelling too."

"And set a bad example to your parrot."

His mother imitated Great Uncle Percy getting excited. "Get on with it, you dozy lump! Faster! Go, go, *go!*"

His father joined in. "Quickly!" he shouted. "Stop hanging about like –"

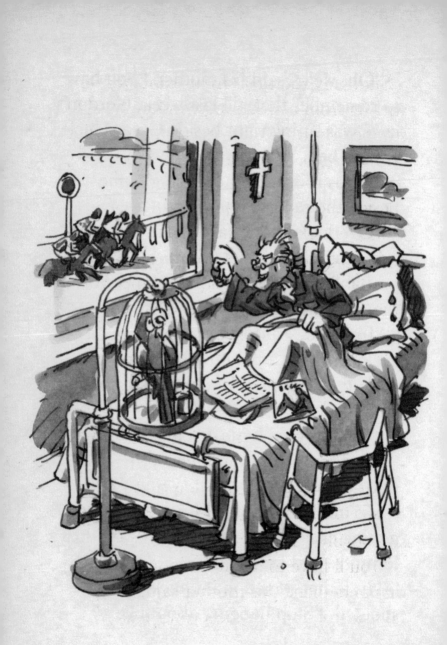

Suddenly spotting Great Aunt Ada waving from a glistening window, he stopped short. "Well," he said, somewhat embarrassed. "I'm sure you get the idea."

Rupert's mouth had dropped open. "Horses!" he was saying. "*Horses?* Are you telling me Great Uncle Percy was just shouting at racehorses?"

"Not really shouting at them," said his mother. "More just urging them on, really."

"Encouraging them loudly."

"Hoping they'd win."

"See?" said his father. "Not really rude at all."

"He called them 'Absolute rubbish!' when they didn't win," Rupert insisted stubbornly. "That's pretty rude."

"You'll have to teach Gordon better manners then," his mother said. "Because I'm afraid he's yours now."

10 Good Manners Are
Like Measles

RUPERT STARED AT his mother. "*Mine?*
Great Uncle Percy has left Gordon to
me?"

His mother sighed heavily. "So it
seems."

She didn't sound delighted.

Rupert considered. On the one hand, it
would be interesting to have a parrot.
Something to talk about at school. But,
on the other hand, it would be horribly
upsetting for Roly. He'd probably spend
his whole time cowering under the bed.
He'd be absolutely terrified.

And that would be an awful shame, now he was trying so hard. He was almost perfect at "Sit!" and "Be quiet!" and "Roll over!". And they were just about to start on "Fetch!" together. It would be such a pity if all the rest of Roly's training was spoiled because of that rude parrot.

"Can I ask Great Aunt Ada if she'll keep Gordon for me? And I could see him when I come and visit her again."

"Visit her again?"

"Yes," Rupert said firmly. (After all, saying hello to a parrot couldn't take long. He'd still have time to learn to make kaleidoscopes. And, even when she'd taught him that, he wouldn't mind still coming. Now he looked back, he realized he'd really enjoyed his day with Great Aunt Ada.)

"Yes," he repeated. "I'd really like to come again. I would look forward to it."

His father put his hands on Rupert's shoulders and turned him round.

Great Aunt Ada was standing there.

"Go on then," said his father. "Ask."

"Please," said Rupert. "Please, Great Aunt Ada, will you keep Gordon for me, and let me visit? Often?"

Great Aunt Ada looked pleased.

"I'd be delighted," she told him. "If you think that's best for Gordon."

"Oh yes," said Rupert. "I do think

that's best for him. Especially if he has to learn good manners."

As they strolled up the path into the house, to finish the cake and tell Gordon, Rupert explained to his parents.

"You see, good manners are like measles. To get them, you really have to go where they already are."

He made a little face. "So it's probably

better for me too, don't you think, to keep on visiting?"

His parents laughed. And Great Aunt Ada winked. Rupert tried winking back. But that was one of the things he wasn't very good at yet.

Perhaps she'd teach him that as well, next time he visited.

He'd come soon.